Grazia Deledda

*Legends of Sardinia*

Edited by Carlo Mulas

English translation of:

Grazia Deledda, *Fiabe e leggende sarde.*

**ISBN 978-88-98737-51-2**



Indibooks



*Cover: Antonio Ballero*

*Sa Ria, 1908*

Grazia Deledda

# *Legends of Sardinia*

Edited by Carlo Mulas

Translated from Italian and Sardinian to English

by Carlo Mulas and the Indibooks Crew.

## Sardinian Legends in "Art and Nature"

*Contos de fuchile* (fireside tales), this sweet name that evokes all the warm serenity of long family evenings spent by the paternal fireplace, is what we call fairy tales, legends and all those fabulous and wonderful stories that are lost in the mists of times other than our own.

The Sardinian people, especially in the wild mountains and desolate plateaus, where the landscape is mysterious and legendary, with its silent, deserted lines or the intense shadows of the steep woods, are very imaginative, full of bizarre and endless superstitions.

In their poverty, the people are made to believe that there are immense treasures hidden beneath their poor feet. Listening to vague rumours, whispered in hushed tones, with trembling accents and a gleam in their eyes, they believe that the whole island is littered with gold coins and precious pearls.

Every mountain, country church, castle ruin, forest and cave hide its treasure.

Placed by whom? If you ask this question, you will get plausible explanations.

There is a vague memory of the wars, raids and plundering that Sardinia has suffered throughout the ages, especially from the Saracens, Goths and Vandals, and it is said that our very ancient ancestors hid their treasures - money, jewels and precious stones - in impenetrable places to protect them from the invaders, and that most of these treasures, which were hidden by the will or against the will of their first owners, still exist today.

Up to this point, the natural.

The supernatural is the radically entrenched belief that the devil watches over treasures: the devil who, if at the end of a certain time people have not found the treasure, takes it for himself and takes it to hell, leaving a lot of coal or ashes in the amphorae or coffins containing the gold and pearls.

The legend of the treasure is so deeply rooted in our culture that as soon as a person succeeds in acquiring a fortune through hard work and intelligence, or perhaps through deceit and perversity, the voice of the people claims that he has found an aschisòrgiu (a treasure).

A thousand memories come to mind, and I recall many events from my childhood. Even somewhat cultured and unscrupulous people believe in treasures without admitting it, and more than one owner unknowingly excavates his land in search of these wonderful riches.

Fairy tales and legends are based on hidden treasures, and ancient traditions point to mysterious places in our mountains where gold is undoubtedly mined.

But often these places - rocks or caves - are viewed with a vague dread by even the strongest and bravest men, whose guns have taken more than one revenge. It is the subtle fear of the supernatural, the terror of things that cannot be conquered by gun or dagger.

Because, as I said, it is believed that many aschisorjos are guarded by the devil, in which case the place is deadly and bad luck befalls those who enter it.

Examples abound. There are men who died of iron shortly after spending a night in one of these caves; shepherds who lost their entire flock to a mysterious disease; bandits whose bones were found to be nothing more than those plucked from eagles and hawks; young men sentenced to life imprisonment. All because they lived near these deadly places.

More than one old shepherd who has miraculously escaped misfortune claims to have seen the devil in human or animal form.

In the small mountains of Nuoro, the green and granite mountains of Orthubene [Ortobene], which are perhaps the most beautiful in Logudoro, there is a mysterious and deep cave, the dark immensity of which, it is said, no one has ever been able to explore.

A shepherd once tried to visit it all the way but saw the demons and fled. Over there is an immense treasure, billions and billions of golds and pearls, and a little lady who always weaves gold, with a gold loom, dressed in gold and with golden hair, guards it.

Oh, little golden lady!

How often have I seen her in my childhood dreams, with her shining train and her sunny hair!

Devils play an important role in Sardinian legends: even in fairy tales they play an important role, and in some they are the main heroes.

However, the Sardinians, being good Christians, always give the spirit of hell a disgusting and often ridiculous place, thus avenging the terror and fear that the devil inspires.

Without dwelling on the superstitions of the Sardinian people, I will now turn to the legends, I would even say historical legends, that run from village to village, from mountain to mountain.

Some are long and frightening, others are short, vague, without a strong outline, but all have a kind of warm southern or Mediterranean atmosphere.

## Sas nurras and the Devil-deer

In the Oliena mountains, the limestone buttresses have sharp peaks. They are milky blue and merge with the sky. There are large crevasses here, reminders of ancient volcanic convulsions, some of which are impossible to tell the bottom of. They are called "sas nurras". The people believe that they are mysterious channels that connect hell with our world. From there the devils come out to roam the white mountains in search of souls and adventure.

Among other legends concerning the nurras, I found this one, very bizarre, and, it seems, not very old.

Once upon a time there was a shepherd from Oliena, very pious and devout. For this reason, he was cursed by the devil, who, when all temptations failed to lead him to evil, took revenge on him in this way.

On a quieter day, the shepherd entrusted the sheep to one of his companions and went into the mountains to hunt deer and mouflon.

It was a beautiful winter's day. He saw a magnificent deer not far from him. He shot at the animal and slightly wounded it. But he could not catch it. So, he went looking for it. The deer jumped from cliff to cliff, very fast, but the shepherd, no less agile, stayed in its tracks, determined to kill it. So they reached the top of the mountain.

The snow covered the peaks, the rocks, the abysses, but the hunter, who knew the places, continued his hunt without stumbling over a single stone, fascinated by the wonderful, beautiful deer, whose auburn antlers were more than six palms high.

Suddenly the animal disappeared, suddenly sinking into the snow. The hunter reached the spot and found himself on the edge of a frighteningly deep nurra.

The deer was no longer visible, but from the depths of the nurra rose a sinister echo of infernal laughter. The wretched shepherd then realised that the deer was the devil himself and tried to flee, but the snow on which he was standing collapsed and before he had made the sign of the cross, he fell into the immensity of the abyss...

His companion had been waiting for him for two days, and he feared some misfortune. So, he set off into the mountains to rescue him.

When he saw the wretch's footprints in the snow, he realised that his mate had met a bad end.

He returned to the village. Then, with a large amount of rope, he and three other shepherds set off for the nurra. Once there, they tied themselves with ropes. Then, having tied the hunter's mate to his armpits, the other men lowered him into the nurra. But no matter how long the ropes were, the man never touched the bottom. The shepherds pulled him up and when he came out, his face was red, and he was trembling.

A deep fear gripped him. But at first, he was reluctant to reveal why. Carried on his shoulders by his comrades, he returned to his home, but no sooner had he arrived than he was seized by a raging fever that led him to his grave three days later...

Before he died, he revealed the mysterious cause of his fear. As he descended into the nurra, a small black man appeared. He had horns and a scythe in his hand. At one point the devil stretched his scythe towards the rope, threatening to break it and throw the shepherd and his mate into hell!

## Legends of Aggius in Gallura

At the end of the 17th century, in Aggius, a small village in Gallura, a boy and a girl, children of two rival families, fell in love, as often happens in Sardinia and elsewhere.

She was thirteen and he was fifteen. They were strong and beautiful. And although they were so young, they looked twenty years old. They loved each other madly, with all the unbridled passion of the people of Gallura.

Gallura is a bizarre mountainous region in the north of Sardinia, with a landscape and wildlife very similar to neighbouring Corsica.

As I said, the families of the two lovers were enemies.

In fact, the entire village was divided into two factions. One faction belonged to the young man's family, the other to the girl's. A deadly hatred burned between them. This did not stop them from worshipping each other and holding frequent nightly meetings in the same house as her.

They used the utmost caution and vigilance, but eventually they were discovered, and her father, burning with rage and hatred, slaughtered the wretched lover on the holy Easter night.

The enmity between the two factions grew deep. And so, the war began! The people of Aggius, lined up on a small plain below the rocky and desolate mountains, armed with guns and daggers, were about to fight when the first shot, fired by the father of the poor girl, caused a terrible rumble that echoed throughout Gallura.

The mountains had collapsed, falling on the cursed warriors, and burying them under huge boulders from which no one could pull them out. Only a few people escaped: old men, women and children who had not taken part in the battle. The cause of this ruin, apart from the innocent one of the two young lovers, was the devil who lived on the mountain peaks. And here I copy from Enrico Costa's sad and trembling novel, *Il muto di Gallura.*

He, the devil, peered between the granite boulders to observe the village below. On those ominous days, a very strong wind could be heard blowing. Although it came from the east, an icy breeze blew from the snow-covered Mount Limbara. And while the people of Aggius felt their bodies chill, the devil was blowing on their souls, stirring up thoughts of hatred, revenge and blood!

It is said that the people of Aggius were originally of a serene and peaceful disposition. But the infernal spirit that sought to damn their souls had taken up residence in the granite palace that stood at the top of the mountain, and rejoiced in the sleepless nights that tormented these poor souls.

The old women trembled in their beds with fear. They recited the rosary under their blankets as the furious wind howled through the cracks in the windows. It was the Son of Hell who, unable to sleep, amused himself by disturbing the sleep of the children of the earth.

He emerged from the cliff. After announcing his presence with a long, dull roll, he shouted three times to the village: "Aggius meu, Aggius meu, e candu sarà la di chi ti n'aggiu a pultà in buleu?" [My Aggius, my Aggius, when will the day come when I will take you away in a whirlwind?]

The infernal threat foretold the destruction of the land, and the long roll that preceded it meant that a man was destined to die a violent death.

At least that is what tradition says.

Imagine the consternation of the population!

The parish priest was called in and the wise men of the village were consulted, but always in vain!

The devil did not give up and continued.

Towards the middle of the 18th century, a zealous missionary who happened to be in Aggius, erected an iron cross on the mountain, later called Monti di la Cruzi (the Mountain of the Cross), to drive away the devil.

That night the wind blew very hard. It uprooted the ancient oaks and caused many granite boulders to fall from the mountain. All the houses shook from their foundations, but the cross stood firm on the top of the mountain.

When the people heard this infernal noise, they ran to the rector, who sent them all home and said to them: "Do not be afraid; it is the devil who is packing his bags to go back to hell. He will no longer come to torment us!"

However, it seems that the devil did not want to give up the souls of the villagers. He had indeed left the Monti di la Cruzi, perhaps to seek refuge on the Monti Fraile or Monti Pinna. From where, as in the past, he continued to pour poison into the souls of the good people of Aggius. And they, in turn, continued to kill each other, spreading terror throughout Gallura.

The Missionary Cross is located on a huge, almost isolated rock. It is twenty to thirty metres high. It gives shape to the top of the mountain, battered by lightning and wind. Originally made of iron, it stood there for more than half a century until one day, struck by lightning, it was replaced by a wooden cross that is renewed every two or three years.

Other legends of Aggius.

The Conca della Madonna is a natural niche dug into the rock. It is said that the Virgin Mary sometimes lived there to keep away the spirit of darkness.

The large drum, Su Tamburu Mannu, is a large slab of granite with a convex base that rests on top of a flattened block.

All you must do is step up to the edge and apply force with your body so that the stone swings, sways, and produces a dark, dull, continuous roll, like the bellowing of thunder in the distance.

The great drum of Aggius has much in common with the famous dancing stone of Nuoro.

There is only one difference: the latter has not danced for many years, while the former continues to play because there are very few curious people who try it.

In the memory of the elders, this drum has always existed, and I do not know what evil influences are still attached to it. It is said, for example, that if you hear it roll, it is a sure sign that a person has died or is about to die a violent death!

## Legends of Castel Doria

The legends surrounding Castel Doria are interesting, especially those of the last prince. It seems that this mysterious castle was built by the Doria family around 1102, when the Genoese were fortifying all their possessions in the north of the island. The most famous of these is Castelsardo.

There is also a tall tower with five corners. It is made of rectangular stones welded together with cement. Built on high cliffs not far from the banks of the river Coghinas, the castle overlooked a magnificent panorama and the green plain at its feet.

Legend has it that an underground passage led from the castle to the church of San Giovanni di Viddacuia, on the other side of the Coghinas, and that the Doria family dug this dungeon to go to mass on feast days. A footpath leads from the tower to the Conca di la Muneta, where the Doria family is said to have minted money.

It is said that this Conca was a large cistern of immense depth. At the bottom there was a golden bell that was rung by throwing a stone.

For this reason, the cistern is now filled to the bottom with stones so that the bell is invisible and no longer rings.

Legend has it that once upon a time, before the stones filled the bottom of the cistern, a man went down and found a door that led to four large and mysterious underground rooms. In one he found a golden staff, and in another he saw a great iron door locked. This door was supposed to lead to other dungeons where the Dorias kept their immense treasures and minted coins. But the explorer could not even move the iron door, nor could anyone open it after the death of the last castellan. So, the treasures are still there!

It is said that there were high walls and large trees to the west of the castle.

The castellans strolled in the shade of the trees in the lazy hours of their battle-hardened existence. And they dreamed, especially in the blue evenings perfumed by the hay of the plain and the rushes of the melancholy Coghinas. And all this - the underground tunnel that leads to San Giovanni di Viddacuia, the mint with its iron gates and the high bastion with its trees - is linked to the legend of the last prince. His name was Andrea Doria, according to the people of Gallura.

Perhaps he was the strong admiral who, in 1527, regained the possessions occupied by the Spaniards and who, according to legend, died in such a strange way.

So, while the prince was spending the winter in the castle, a lady, wife or daughter, I do not know, of a knight in the service of the Dorias, who lived in the same castle, fell madly in love with Andrea. But no matter how many pleasantries and enthusiastic declarations she made to him, he never wanted to hear them.

Once, angered by the woman's advances, he rudely rebuffed her. He was a gentle knight, but he lost his patience. So, he threatened to throw the woman out of the castle.

She was burning with love, but also with hate. So, the woman went to see a famous Corsican witch.

The witch lived on the top of a mountain. From these desolate rocks, she ruled the two neighbouring islands - Corsica and Sardinia - with her magic.

"My lady," said the witch, "there is nothing I can do for you. The knight is devoted to St. John, and St. John protects him from love spells. No filter and no magic can touch his heart. But I can put you in touch with someone who knows more than I do!"

The lady accepted.

The witch then took her to the devil. In exchange for her noble soul, he gave her the power of transformation, incantation, and witchcraft. Invaded by the infernal spirit, the lady tried every trick in the book to win Andrea Doria's love, but St John protected the knight from guilty love, and so her last flatteries were in vain.

Then love turned to hate and the lady turned to perversion.

One day she changed her face into that of an old woman, disguised herself as a witch and entered the dungeon that led from the castle to the church.

And as the prince was going to church, the witch stopped him and said, "Sir, Saint John of Viddacuia has sent me to tell you: beware, a great disaster is upon you! The day you see the fields of Coghinas covered with horses and green riders, that day your castle will be conquered. You and your court will be hanged by the neck from the walls of Castel Doria!"

Then she disappeared.

There is no telling what astonishment and vague fear filled the souls of the knights at such an arcane prophecy.

A great melancholy seized Andrea Doria.

He fortified the castle but was sure of victory. Nevertheless, he sent the keys to the dungeon where the treasures were to his sister who lived in Genoa. Trusting in God and St John, he waited.

The perfidious woman, meanwhile, worked...

It was May.

The Coghinas' fields were covered with asphodel and tall hay. It was then that the witch worked her magic.

In one night, she turned all the asphodel stalks and pliant stalks of fresh hay into green horses, ridden by warriors armed with green shields and spears, dressed in green tunics and armour!

At dawn, when Andrea Doria stepped out onto the ramparts to breathe in the fresh breeze of the floral dawn, he turned deathly pale.

And he saw!

He saw his castle besieged by this green and immense army that stretched to the horizon. He felt that in a short time this great and mysterious enemy, coming suddenly from unknown lands - without the messengers and heralds who had been sent to all the Italian and foreign courts to warn him if any army was on the move, without having given any alarm - would invade and defeat his fortress. And the terrible prophecy of the witch came back to him: "You will be hanged by the neck from the battlements of Castel Doria!"

Never! Never! Never! Better to die bravely!

And indeed, as the green army grew more numerous and threatening, the brave prince leapt from the ramparts and died, crushed to the rocks below!

He was dead.

The green army was gone.

Only fields of asphodel and hay.

A devilish laugh echoed in the cool silence of the blue morning. It was the sad laughter of a cursed soul.

The witch had taken her revenge.

On hearing of her brother's death, the sister from Genoa, who held the keys to the treasures and the mint, set sail for Sardinia to open the vaults and transport the treasures to the continent, but at sea she was seized by a terrible illness.

Foreseeing his death, he let himself be carried on deck, and in his agony threw the keys into the sea, his dying eyes fixed on the fatal and fascinating distant island where his beloved and unfortunate brother lay asleep.

She died too.

Buried among the emerald tombs of the Mediterranean, no one has been able to open the Conca di la Muneta. That is why the treasures of the Dorias still shine there, in the shadows of the underground.

Many years after Andrea's death, a shepherd spending the night near Castel Doria saw an illuminated door on the wall of the bastion. He entered and saw a magnificent and immense hall. It was filled with fabrics, canvases, brocades, jewels, furniture, flowers, statues, crystals, pearls, and gold.

Gold, yes. There were also great statues and lighted lamps of gold. A beautiful woman, dressed in a white veil and full of jewels, stood behind an alabaster bench.

"Piddani e lassanni" [catch and release], she said to the shepherd with a sweet smile, pointing at everything. But the fool, remembering that he needed a lot of underwear, took only a piece of cloth, and went away.

He immediately returned to his mother and brothers and told them of his adventure.

That night the whole family set off for Castel Doria.

From a distance they could see the bright light of the wall, but as they got closer it disappeared. At the foot of the castle they saw only the black and sad wall in the silent night!

## The Castle of Galtellì

One night in December, I spent more than two hours listening to a woman from Orosei. She told me the legends of the castle of Galtellì. Her voice was so sincere and her conviction so strong. I often found myself staring at her with an indefinable gasp. And I wondered if there might not be some truth in these bizarre supernatural stories that go round people's houses.

The castle of Galtellì, the Civitas Galtellina, once so prosperous and populous, now reduced to a miserable village, is destroyed. Only the black and desolate ruins remain, dominating the sad village, silent and austere in the mysterious landscape.

I can say that a magical circle of strange and ancient beliefs surrounds these dark ruins.

The most important of these legends is that of the last baron, or rather his ghost, who watches over the castle ruins day and night, guarding its hidden treasures.

By day, the Baron is invisible. But at night, on a calm or stormy night, anyone who dares to visit the ruins will see the Baron walking slowly by. He wanders through the brambles and boulders or along the black walls, remembering the best days of his existence. He is young but has a very sad face. He is dressed in medieval style, with a sword at his side and a vaporous quilted collar around his neck.

What fate condemned him to wander like this? Always, for centuries and centuries, on the ruins of his magnificent mansion, where once joy and splendid power reigned?

Nobody knows. Perhaps it was an excommunication by the Pope, or perhaps it was a malediction. But apart from the Baron, people believe that there are other ghosts in the castle. These ghosts have a human form, wander in the dungeons, and never come out.

These are the members of the last baron's family: his wife, his daughter, his son-in-law and a grandson, the latter born in the strange way I am telling you. As in the legend of Castel Doria, there is said to be an underground passage in this castle that leads very far. For some, it connects this castle to those in the south of the island. For others, it goes all the way to Cagliari, crossing great chains of mountains, rivers, and plains!

The Baron's spirit is peaceful and generous. He has never harmed anyone and has often done good for the poor of the village.

Late one evening, as he was returning from the countryside with wood on his shoulders, a poor village farmer found himself in the dark. So, he stopped for a moment near the ruins of the castle.

It was a very cold night, but the moon was shining brightly. The farmer saw a gentleman walking in the nearby mountains. Curious and brave, the man climbed a little higher to see a strange gentleman walking comfortably in that inhospitable and cold place.

Then the gentleman noticed the man and stopped. He was blond and had a delicate face, with two large, glassy, misty eyes bathed in the pain of an eternal sadness.

"Who are you?", he asked the man in a friendly way.

When the farmer had answered, the gentleman looked at the bundle of wood the man had put in the path. Then he said again, "My daughter and my wife are so cold, so cold! Can you give me your wood?"

"And why not?", exclaimed the farmer, won over by the mysterious gentleman's fine manners. So, he carried the wood to the ruins. But he did not take the reward the gentleman offered.

But soon after this meeting, everyone in the village saw something truly amazing. The farmer bought land and houses and spent as much money as a rich man. In short, he became the richest man in the village. So, to get rid of his reputation as a thief, he told the whole truth.

After that night, he returned to the castle many times, taking all the wood needed for the winter to the invisible spirits who lived in the castle ruins. In return, the Baron gave him many, many sacks of gold!

Then there is the legend, or the apparently more recent tradition, of the Baron's grandson. One night, a woman who lived in the village heard a knock at the door. When she opened it, she saw a magnificently dressed knight, who said to her, "Quick, come with me. You are needed!"

She, who was very poor and had few opportunities to try her luck, did not beg. She dressed and followed the man who walked quickly and quietly in front of her.

They walked through the village and out into the countryside.

The woman asked anxiously, "Where are we going, sir?"

"Come and fear nothing," he said. His voice was so soft and gentle that the woman was reassured and followed him in silence.

The knight led her to the ruins of the castle. Then he took her by the hand and led her to the underground chambers she had heard so much about.

These rooms shone with luxury and splendour. They were covered with tapestries and brocade curtains and furnished like paradise. They were also lighted by great chandeliers of gold and pearls. In one of them there was a very rich bed where a very pale and beautiful young lady lay in terrible suffering.

Another lady, older but also beautiful and graceful, attended him, while a young knight paced frantically from one end of the room to the other.

Some time passed.

And the village woman finally gave the lady a beautiful doll with ribbons and lace and said, "Here is a gracious gift, madam!"

Then the lady, after kissing the child, smiled sadly, and replied, "But he is not of your world, good woman!"

When it was all over, the old knight took the woman by the hand, led her outside and accompanied her to her home.

Left alone, she wondered why she had received no reward from these strange people. But when she opened the door the next morning, she found a large bag of gold coins on the edge.

"That is why," concluded the woman who told me the legends of the castle of Galtellì, "the descendants of that woman are now among the richest in the country!"

## The legend of Our Lady of Gonare

In many Sardinian legends the saints, the Madonna and Jesus himself often play a lively role. There is no Madonna that does not have its own legend. And almost all the churches – especially the small rural churches, the small brown churches lost in the desolate plains or in the solitary mountains, which bear the imprint of Pisan or Andalusian buildings – are surrounded by a simple or legendary tradition.

I will recall two of them below.

The first is the legend of the small church built on top of Mount Gonare, near the village of Orane [Orani], 1120 metres above sea level. Gonare is one of Sardinia's most characteristic mountains, and its blue pyramidal peak can be seen from many places on the island. The small church is built right at the top, a symbolic challenge to lightning, wind, and storms. And that is the legend.

Gonario di Torres, King of Logudoro, once sailed the western seas of Sardinia. Suddenly he was caught in a terrible storm. So, he promised Nostra Signora (Our Lady) that if she would save him, he would build a church on the top of the first mountain he saw. Having promised to do so, the storm seemed to magically die down. Then, beyond the last thinning clouds, on the horizon, the pious Gonario saw a blue mountain, which he was told was near the village of Orane. In the same year, the king had a modest temple built at his own expense, and the mountain was given the name of Gonario, which was gradually reduced to Gonare.

Our Lady so appreciated the king's homage that she came to Sardinia to visit his new temple. As she climbed the steep mountain path, she leaned against a rock to rest.

You can still see the rock with a small groove in it.

According to popular tradition, the groove was left by Our Lady's shoulders. Women devoutly lean against this rock and collect the dust scraped from it. "Leaning against it," they say, "prevents sore shoulders and the dust cures fever!"

When Our Lady came down from Mount Gonare, she met St Barbara and told her:

Barbaredda de Orzai,
Ube tind'ana a ponner
No nor bidimus mai!

[Little Barbara from Olzai, / Where will they put you / We will never see each other!]

In fact, the church of Santa Barbara was built in the village of Olzai, near Gonare, but in a low place. It is therefore not visible from the top of Gonare and does not form part of the wonderful view.

## Saint Peter of Sorres

I found this legend some time ago in a Sardinian literary magazine, La terra dei nuraghes, written by Pompeo Calvia, one of the kindest Sardinian poets. This story is about the church of San Pietro di Sorres, near Torralba, an ancient church that is now almost in ruins. For Calvia, it is the oldest monument of medieval art in the area.

The sweet and mysterious legend tells that in ancient times, perhaps around the year 1000, there lived a young maestro of Sorres, an artist and gentle poet. Back in his country, after studying with a famous painter and architect, the young man found a mysterious window in the village "where roses grew with great grace and abundance, and the bellflowers intertwined with the spirals of the columns". The window never opened, and no one ever appeared among the flowers.

Once a month, a tapestry of stars, figures and laurels waved lightly on the windowsill. But the hand that stretched it out and pulled it back was invisible. Out of curiosity, the young artist asked about this mysterious house, but no one knew anything about it.

The greatest mystery reigned.

Then one night the young man went to listen at the window and heard only the very sweet voice of a woman singing "like a dying swan song" and he also heard the slight movement of the spools of a loom.

Burned with curiosity, the artist took his guitar and sang a sad and passionate song under the mysterious window. Then, when the snow fell and the night was raw, he knocked on the window and asked for asylum, saying he was a lost traveller.

But a gentle voice answered him: " "I have no bread to give you; in my little bed there are only thorns; a thousand and a thousand garnet steps you must climb to reach me, and I seem so near to you. When you arrive, I will be cold as death. Traveller, go away!"

And because he insisted, she advised him to go to the nearby church. But he replied that the church was destroyed, and it was snowing inside. "Then build one," said the voice.

"I will build it if you draw me the project!"

"I will give it to you but go away!"

The voice no longer spoke.

The young man left.

After many months, he saw a magnificent tapestry of a Pisan church embroidered in the window.

The embroidery was magnificent.

It shows the inside of the church with all the details of the interior. The artist understood and carved the drawing in his head. But it took a lot of money to build such a temple, and the country was very poor.

What to do?

The young man was madly in love with the mysterious woman of Sorres, who had suggested that he build the church. He was determined to keep his promise so that he could meet her.

He painted a Madonna in a golden field with an almond tree in her hand. Then he gave his beautiful painting to the old, destroyed church.

Everyone admired the painting, but one morning they saw that the Madonna was holding a church instead of an almond tree. The church was like that of the tapestry.

It was the young man who painted it. In fact, he had sneaked into the old church one night, erased the almond tree and painted the new church.

Everyone was shouting "miracle, miracle". And then, "Our Lady wants a church like this". Then a monk took the miraculous painting and went to the castles, the countryside, and the villas to collect money and offerings for the construction of the new church. And when he had filled many chests with gold, he proposed to the young master of Sorres to build the temple.

He accepted. Then many workmen were called and, in short, despite the evil spirits that destroyed the building every night, the church was built, beautiful and rich as the design of the tapestry!

The night before the consecration, while the whole village was celebrating the great event, animated by the people of the neighbouring villages, the young people went to the mysterious house.

He knocked on the door.

"Who are you?", asked the sweet enchantress.

"I have come to take a flower from your hands and give it to Our Lady," the young man sighed, "Please, open!"

"All right, I'm coming."

The door was magically opened, and the young man found himself in front of the mysterious woman.

She seemed to be dressed in silver, with a black stole over her robe. She had blonde hair on her shoulders and a very pale face that stood out against the embroidery on the walls. The embroidery was constantly changing, forming tapestries of arabesques and perfectly woven and drawn figures. In the centre, the design of the new church remained unchanged.

In the corner stood the golden loom with all its golden threads. The beauty nodded with serene eyes, without change, all composed in the sweetness of the act, like the figures seen in the Byzantine mosaics. She had olive branches at her feet and bay leaves with golden berries in her hands.

She let go of a bay leaf.

He picked it up.

The woman approached him. She was beautiful, just as he had dreamed. The young man moved closer to kiss those divine lips. But no sooner had he kissed her than he felt his exhausted body freeze. Then he fell at her feet and, gazing softly at the woman, died.

## The curse of the monks

There is still a strong belief among the Sardinian people that the excommunication of the Pope, or even of a simple priest, really brings a curse on the excommunicated person and his descendants.

On this subject I found, among others, this legend. In a village near Nuoro there was a rich monastery. The monks who lived there ruled not only over their property and their brothers, but over the whole region and its people. That is why they were so hated. The villagers had pleaded with the Pope to stop the violence. But in Rome there was no time to think about the Sardinian village. It was then that a group of boys, a little reckless and without prejudice, decided to take a few shots at the monks who had discredited them with the Pope and marked their downfall.

Oddly enough, an opportunity favoured the boys.

On a feast day, as solemn ceremonies were being held in the monastery church, a child died suddenly, perhaps the son of one of the conspirators against the monks.

Without telling anyone in the village, the young men took the child's body and threw it into a well in the monastery at night. The next day, the whole village commented on the disappearance of the child, who had been seen the day before, healthy, and happy, walking the corridors of the convent with other children of his age. And after searching, the body was finally found in the well! Imagine the indignation and anger of the people! Because it was said that the child had been killed by the monks, who knows why?

The monks managed to escape, but news of the crime reached the court of the kingdom of Logudoro. The king, in agreement with the Pope, issued a decree: the monastery was to be destroyed and the monks banished.

The monks tried in vain to justify themselves. But their pleas fell on deaf ears in Rome and Ardara, the seat of the king. The monastery was destroyed. Then the rich and powerful monks left. But before they left, they cast their most terrible curses on the villagers and their descendants. The village has been cursed ever since. Plague, famine, unimaginable misfortune has struck it again and again. But not only. Its inhabitants, driven by the deadliest hatred, killed each other.

## The spirit of Madame Galdona

It seems that in Sassari there was a rich lady who was very pious and devout. Her name was Madama Galdona. When she died, she left a farm to the monks. Then the government took it away. So, they cursed the farm. And indeed, all those who bought it, one by one, suffered many misfortunes. And the lady who was the first mistress, or her ghost, wanders among the trees of the farm from time to time, murmuring curses and pleading with the enemies of her beloved heirs.

These are serious and traditional Sardinian legends.

As I have already said, Sardinia has an infinite number of legends, all of them marked by the southern imagination of the peoples who have mixed with us in every age. To collect them all would take up a lot of space, and here I have given just a few examples, chosen from among the shortest, the gentlest and the least intertwined.

## Local legends

Today I would like to tell the spiritual readers of Vita Sarda two charming local legends. Nowadays legends are fashionable, and in the revival of popular studies, to which all thinkers, writers and poets turn their gaze, almost like a cool shore to land on after so many dark literary storms, legend takes first place.

The legend is at once aristocratic, artistic, vulgar, and popular. The refined mind of the cultivated lady and the rough and poetic imagination of the people are attracted to legends. As well as the dreamer's soul of the artist and the unscrupulous and inquisitive perception of the scientist.

The legend concerns the poet and the historian, who use it to find in its trunk the traces of buried generations, the nature of living generations and the germ of future generations. It can arouse the same interest in the gay circles of elegant salons and in the souls of pastors gathered around the sad hearth, in children and adults alike, and can finally provide material for a serious, learned, scientific volume and for a book of pleasant reading, frothy, elegantly useless.

I have studied elsewhere the character of the Sardinian legend which, apart from the sarcastic cycles of legends addressed to a character or a village, has the serious and melancholy profile of the southern traditions.

I will quickly say that Sardinia, a land of legends and mysteries, is full of legends. Every country church, every castle or monastery ruin, every village, every cussorgia (region or area), every cave, every cliff, every mountain and valley has its own legend. Some legends cross and merge with fairy tales - like the first of the two I am going to tell you about today - with the plausible, mixing the fantastic with distant reminiscences of Nordic legends, sagas, Flemish or Alemannian fairy tales, but the best part has a local explanation that clearly shows its character.

The protagonists are historical figures who mingle with devils, fairies, witches and janas; they are the giants who live in the nuraghes; they are the Saracens, the Pisans, the Genoese, the Spaniards, the judges (kings) and the bishops who, at all times after the Roman domination, of which only the Sardinians, who remain so deeply Latin in their customs and language, hardly remember, have done good and evil to the island.

They are the Dorias and the Malaspinas; they are the judges of Torres; the Aragonese viceroys; the monks; the witches who flourished in the Middle Ages; the raids and adventures of the Saracen pirates in the last centuries of the first millennium; unknown artists, perhaps of the fourteenth and fifteenth centuries, not even remembered by the few Sardinian chronicles; mysterious ladies, saints and warriors, and sometimes the same Jesus or Mary.

Many Sardinian legends have a real historical value, especially those of some churches and some mountains. Without the shadow of reverie, without fronds, without supernatural characters, if they were collected and studied, they would be elements or, I would say, living documents, useful for the history of Sardinia.

## The three brothers and the three janas

*This legend was collected in Nurri, a large village in the district of Lanusei, by the kind lady Maria Manca, a scholar of Sardinian customs and traditions.*

In the mountain range that surrounds Nurri, in the mountain called Pala Perdixi or Corongius, there is a natural cave, very large and interesting, where farmers and shepherds go to rest and sometimes spend the night. Once upon a time, three brothers, three good villagers, tired after picking olives all day, entered this cave in the evening to rest. While they were peacefully discussing rural matters and eating bread and dripping, they saw three women entering the cave, who stopped at the entrance and looked at them suspiciously.

Being the good young men they were, they kindly invited them to join them for dinner. The women accepted. Then, after the meal, they asked the three workers who they were.

"We are three orphan brothers," they replied with grace, "and we work to live. We are so poor. If we could improve our situation, we would do it immediately."

The three women were three witches, or rather three fairies, called orgianas or janas. First, they consulted with their eyes. Then they seemed to combine something, communicating in a strange language that sounded more like a meow. Then the elder fairy took a tablecloth from her pocket and gave it to the elder brother, saying, "Good young man, take this gift, which I give you as a true friend. Whenever you want to eat, you and your brothers and the whole company need only beat this tablecloth three times and then lay it down wherever you like. And all good things will appear to you above it."

The second fairy turned to her second brother and offered him a purse, saying, "And you take this. Each time you open it, you will find money according to your will."

The youngest, meanwhile, gave the third a kind of wind instrument called the leoneddas or launeddas and said: "This wind instrument I am giving you will be of use not only to you, but to all those who will play it and hear it. Go, dear child, I have nothing better, but you will see that this humble gift will be of greater use to you than the tablecloth and the purse they give to your brothers".

After all this, the brothers and the fairies greeted each other warmly and said the ritual "teneis accontu" (good luck) of the southern Sardinians. The three boys, owners of these wonderful talismans, no longer needed to work and began to travel around the island's towns in search of adventure and pleasure.

Wherever they went, they left traces of charity and generosity, good boys that they were. But one day a powerful priest ordered them to stop using their talismans, on pain of excommunication and imprisonment.

Here (I open a parenthesis) the legend does not speak clearly, but probably this piece is a vague memory of the Inquisition, established in Sardinia in the middle of the fifteenth century, but also practised before that by some friars and imported, of course, from Spain.

The three brothers laughed at the priest's warning.

The talismans were invisible to everyone. Only the three brothers could see them. So, they had nothing to fear.

In the face of the priest's constant threats, the youngest of the brothers began to play. The leoneddas had the power to make all those who heard his music dance, except for the three brothers. Even the priest, against his will, began to dance to a ridiculous and uncontrollable rhythm.

Many people came. As soon as they heard the magical sound, they began to dance, unable to stop. Soon the street was full of people who seemed mad, jumping, climbing, and writhing, begging the mysterious performer to stop. But he was amused to see the priest, fat, and round, suffering more than the others in this infernal dance. And he didn't stop until he saw him fall, exhausted.

After all this, the three brothers fled. But soon they were found together, tied up and thrown to the bottom of a tower. But even on the tower they enjoyed playing, dancing, and eating with the other prisoners and guards. So, their trial was soon over. After a few days they were sentenced to death and taken to the gallows. A huge crowd of people, even from far away countries, had come to see the spectacle of the hanging of the three sorcerers.

Before dying, each of the three brothers asked the judges for a last wish. The condemned were not denied any final grace except that of life, so the three brothers got what they asked for.

The first asked to offer lunch to the whole audience, including the judges. The proposal was enthusiastically accepted, and the young man laid his tablecloth on the stage. All kinds of food, fruit, sweets, and exquisite wines appeared on the strange table. People ate and drank again and again. And the more food and drink they consumed, the more they appeared on the table. In short, all the guards, executioners, people, and magistrates were drunk and full to the brim.

Then the second brother expressed his desire to give money. And of course, it was granted! The boy opened the magic purse and distributed huge sums of money in coins and notes (there were no bank notes yet) to those poor devils of soldiers, peasants and shepherds who had never seen such a miracle.

While everyone was going crazy with joy - as we would have done ourselves, despite our seriousness and noble disdain for money - the third brother asked to play the leoneddas. The judges and the crowd, hoping for one last favour, agreed.

The boy, standing on the fatal stage, began to play. Immediately all the drunken crowd, the judges, the soldiers and the executioners began a furious and macabre dance, pushing, punching, bumping, falling to the ground, who fainted, who was injured and who even died. And in the terrible confusion, the three brothers managed to escape and save themselves with their talismans.

## The legend of Monte Bardia

This legend dates to the 8th or 9th century.

After the revolt of the Sardinians against the Byzantine domination, who had fled from the weak Greeks of Cagliari, the island held out for a while, ruled by the famous king Gialeto, who had already been the leader of the revolutionaries. But it was invaded by the Saracens, who devoured it with all kinds of raids, pillages, and disasters.

The coasts of the island were always full of pirates and Saracen warriors, and the maritime villages certainly suffered the most. The people of Dorgali, a large village in the district of Nuoro, near the east coast but defended by a high limestone mountain, always kept a group of strong and brave men on the crest of the mountain to guard against any movements of the Saracens camped on the coast below.

It was a siege. The Saracens waited for the moment when they could safely pass through the mountains, but the Dorgalians guarded them. Time passed in vain as the Saracens made a false retreat. Deceived and driven by their deep religious faith, the Dorgalian guards left the mountain on a solemn feast day and went down to the village to attend the sacred services. The Saracens disembarked and climbed the mountain. As they were about to descend into the village, they stopped in fear and looked on.

They saw a long line of people dressed in bright colours, carrying strange white sticks, crosses, clubs, and flags, marching through the streets of Dorgali. They seemed to be heading for the mountain.

It was a procession. But thanks to Our Lady, who saw it from above and from afar, the Saracens thought the procession was an army preparing to hunt them down and kill them. So, they fled quickly, and one of them was hanged from the trees on the mountain. One of them, I think, is still called the Saracen tree. This is the gentle legend of the mountains of Dorgali, immortalised by one of the main peaks, which, in memory of this fact, is called "of the guard" (de sa Bardia).

## The story of Don Juanne and Mariedda

Today, my little friends, I want to tell you a story that will move you very much. And if it does not move you, it will certainly not be because of me or the things I tell you, but because you have hearts of stone.

Once upon a time in Sardinia, in a village where you have never been and perhaps never will be, there was a bad man who did not believe in God and never gave alms to the poor.

This man was called Don Juanne Perrez, because he was of Spanish origin, and he was ugly as the devil. He lived in a huge, black, and mysterious house with a hundred and one rooms. To serve him, he had a fifteen-year-old niece called Mariedda. She was as good, beautiful, and pious as her uncle was bad, ugly, and excommunicated. Mariedda also had the most beautiful black hair in all of Sardinia. Her eyes were like the morning and evening stars.

Don Juanne hated Mariedda. As he hated all the people in the world. If he could, he would have gouged out her pretty eyes, but he did not. Maybe he still had a shred of conscience. But when she turned fifteen, he tried to get rid of her. So, he arranged a marriage with an ugly man from the village, called Predu Concaepreda (Peter Head of Stone). But she did not accept the unhappy marriage.

One night, in revenge for the humiliating refusal, the ugly man from the village uprooted all the plants in Don Juanne's garden. Then he placed a pair of horns and two huge pumpkins in front of her house. Every night he passed under the windows and sang dirty songs. It is impossible to describe Don Juanne's anger and dislike for poor Mariedda.

A few days later, he took her to the most secluded room in the house and said: "You didn't want to marry Predu Concaepreda. All right, but you have to get married, so get ready to marry me".

The poor girl was stunned, then exclaimed, "But how does this thing work? You are my uncle! And uncles cannot marry nieces!"

"Shut up, you wretch! I can marry who I want, even without a priest. The Pope gave it to me. You must mind your own business. Choose either this man from the village or me. I give you one night to decide." And he left, locking her in.

Alone, Mariedda began to cry and prayed fervently to Nostra Signora del Buon Consiglio for help and inspiration.

That night, Mariedda saw a beautiful woman appear. She was surrounded by light and dressed in satin. She wore a white veil, a blue mantle, and a gold diadem like that of the Queen of Spain.

Where had she come from?

Mariedda could not explain it. She looked at the beautiful woman with her mouth open as she spoke to her in a voice that sounded like violin music: "I am Nostra Signora del Buon Consiglio, and I have heard your prayer. Listen, Mariedda: ask your uncle for eight days. If in that time he has not changed his mind, call on me again. Be of good cheer and you will never lack for my help and advice."

After speaking, she disappeared, leaving the room with moonlight and the scent of jasmine.

Mariedda felt great joy and prayed all night. The next day, she asked her uncle for eight days. Although reluctant, Don Juanne agreed.

To keep her from running away, he locked her in that remote room where there was still moonlight and the smell of jasmine.

But after eight days he asked her if she had made up her mind. He was determined to marry her the very next day.

Alone, Mariedda began to cry and pray again. Immediately the Celestial Lady appeared. She wore a dress of gold brocade and a diadem of pearls like that of the Queen of France.

"Sleep, Mariedda, and do not be afraid," she said in a voice that sounded like the music of a nightingale. "Take this rosary, which has the virtue of healing the sick. And when you are happy, do not forget me if you do not want to be unhappy."

Then she disappeared, leaving a spring dawn light and the scent of carnations in the room.

Mariedda could not say a word.

Full of hope and ecstasy, she kissed the mother-of-pearl rosary that the Celestial Lady had given her. Then she put it on and fell asleep peacefully, not wondering what would happen the next day.

The next day she woke up under a bush near a swamp. She thought that the Blessed Mother had taken her there while she was asleep.

She got up and said the usual prayer. Then she walked towards a town she could see in the distance, surrounded by the rosy vapours of the beautiful morning.

As she walked, she saw a fisherman. He had bare feet and a line over his shoulder because he fished in the small blue ponds in the area.

She asked: "Gentle fisherman, please, what is the name of this town?"

And the fisherman began to sing:

"Io pesco anguilla, e do la caccia all'oca;

quella città laggiù si chiama Othoca".

[I fish eel, and I hunt goose.

That town over there is called Othoca.]

"Well," Mariedda thought, "I'm in Oristano."

She entered the city. She looked for a house where she could work as a servant. But it was all in vain.

For three days and nights she knocked on every door. She was hungry and exhausted. And she had found no work. But she did not despair. She prayed; she always prayed to the beautiful Signora del Buon Consiglio to help her.

On the fourth day, as she passed in front of the royal palace, she saw people talking softly, pale and in pain.

"Gentle soldier," she asked a young gunner, who was as sad as the rest of the crowd, "what is going on?"

"The son of the Judge of Arboréa is dying, and no doctor can save him."

The Judge was the King of Arboréa. Therefore, his son was the royal prince and the most handsome knight in all of Sardinia.

Mariedda was shocked at the news. She was about to say a Hail Mary for the dying prince when, touching the beads of her rosary, she happily remembered that it had the virtue of healing the sick.

Silently, she passed through the crowd and sneaked into the royal palace. But a captain of the guards stopped her and arrogantly asked her what she wanted.

"I am here to heal Don Mariano, the sick prince," she replied humbly. "I have a miraculous medicine that can cure even the dying."

Then the arrogant captain took her to the Judge, an old man with a beard down to his knees, to whom she repeated his words.

The King was astonished by the beautiful little stranger, especially by what she said.

So, he said, "Beware, girl with eyes like a star. If you deceive us, we will cut off your head."

"And if I save the prince?"

"We will give you what you want."

With these words, the King took Mariedda to the dying prince.

Time was running out.

Just a second and all was lost.

Then she placed the rosary around the prince's neck. Then, kneeling on the deerskin spread out in front of the bed, she prayed fervently.

At that moment, the people in the room, white in the face and amazed, saw an extraordinary miracle. Don Mariano opened his beautiful brown eyes with their long lashes. Gradually his cheeks became as rosy as the blossoms of the oleanders in the Royal Gardens; his forehead glowed with life; he smiled; he stood up and said, "Father, I am risen. Who has saved me?"

The Judge wept for joy. He wept so much that his beard dripped with tears like a tree wet from the rain.

"There!" he replied, lifting Mariedda up in his arms.

"You must be a fairy," the prince said, embracing her. "Your eyes have moonlight inside... You shall be my bride."

Soon after, brocade gowns full of gold and silver arrived from France and Flanders for the wedding. So Mariedda became Giudicessa of Arboréa. She was so happy that she forgot the advice of Nostra Signora del Buon Consiglio; she forgot to pray and to remember her always, even when she was happy.

After a year, Mariedda had completely forgotten her saintly patroness. The miraculous rosary was hung in the Royal Chapel, together with other relics. Now Giudicessa rarely went to the chapel. She spent her time at parties, hunts, tournaments and among the songs, lutes, and mandolins of the court troubadours.

One day, the Spanish invaded the kingdom of Arboréa. So, Don Mariano, Mariedda's husband, had to leave with his army to defend his lands and repel the invaders. He left just as she was pregnant with a little prince.

"Goodbye, my love," he said, kissing her forehead. Then, before riding off on his white horse dressed in red, he added: "Strength and courage. When I return, I will find a new little prince, beautiful and strong, like..."

"Like you, my love!" replied Donna Mariedda proudly.

During the war, Don Mariano spent a long time away from his capital, from his old father and from his love.

A couple of months after he left, he became the father of a beautiful baby. The child had rose skin. His little feet and hands looked like flowers. But someone was anxiously awaiting the day of the birth of the beautiful child who would destroy all the happiness of the Giudicessa Mariedda.

It was Don Juanne Perrez.

Listen to me.

After his niece's disappearance, he began to hate her bitterly and cried out for revenge. He looked for her in the Logudoro and all over northern Sardinia. But no one had ever seen or heard of the girl with eyes like stars. So, the wicked Don Juanne believed that the devil had taken her away. When he went to Oristano for the prince's wedding, he was surprised and angry to see that the bride was Mariedda!

What did he do then?

He went back to his village and sold everything he owned. He even sold his soul to the devil to conduct his vendetta (revenge). So, he dressed up as a doctor, with a long white beard and a black cymar. He dressed as Claudius Galen, the ancient doctor, as he had read in an old book.

Disguised as a doctor, Don Juanne Perrez returned to Oristano. Here he said that he had just arrived from Germany and that he had studied in Regensburg. So, he became a court physician.

Mariedda did not recognise him.

When the child was born, the doctor was called. Don Juanne had been waiting for this opportunity to take his own revenge. He hid the baby and replaced it with an ugly, mangy little black dog. He did this cowardly job with such *mastery* that not even Mariedda noticed.

Don Juanne did not kill the child but left him to starve. This is why in Sardinia the Hunger is still called Monsiù Juanne, in memory of this event.

Meanwhile, all the people of the Royal Court were grieving and frightened. In fact, no one had ever seen anything like it. And Mariedda fell ill with grief and humiliation.

Mon Dieu! A little black dog, ugly and mangy, born of a commoner, was not a problem. Why? Well, in those days there were witches who married the devil so that they could also give birth to dogs and scorpions. But for a Giudicessina, dressed in brocade full of gold and silver, it was quite different. It was just too much! So, a letter was sent to Don Mariano who, for the first time in his life, wept with grief.

Mariano may have forgiven Mariedda. But the news spread among the Spaniards. The enemies mocked the prince. Then he became very angry. He wrote to his Maggiordomo and ordered him to take the Giudicessina and her little monster to a faraway place. He rejected her and never wanted to see her again.

Thus, the Maggiordomo executed the order.

One night he took poor Mariedda far away, to a deserted and silent region. She held the little dog in her arms. She still loved him with all her heart.

Alone and desperate in that deserted and silent land, she finally remembered her past; she remembered Nostra Signora del Buon Consiglio.

She fell to the ground crying and asked "perdono."

As in the dark room of Don Juanne's house, she saw a great golden light. Then, the Madonna appeared in her white dress, with the blue mantle and the diadem like that of the Queen of Spain.

"Mariedda, Mariedda," she said, with a very sweet voice that comforted the poor afflicted, "you have forgotten me.

That is why misfortune has struck you. But I leave no one alone because I am the Mother of the afflicted."

With her face to the ground, Mariedda was in tears and prayer. "Mariedda," said the Mother again, "go, and you will find a house where you will have everything you need. Stay there until the time is right. And never forget me."

Having said all this, she disappeared.

The rising sunlight spread across the desolate land. The bushes blossomed and the streams glistened. A sweet scent of mint wafted through the air as the blackbird sang from a wall. When she rose from the floor, Mariedda no longer found the black dog in her arms, but the child with rosy skin, tiny feet and little hands. For a moment she thought of returning to court with the beautiful child. But then she remembered the words of Nostra Signora del Buon Consiglio. So, she walked on across the vast plain that suddenly bloomed.

She walked and walked and walked. After hours and hours, she found a beautiful green house hidden in a grove of oranges and roses. Great golden globes fell from the trees, while great coral flowers sprouted from the bushes.

Mariedda knocked on the door.

A maid in costume, with a fiery scarlet skirt, a green and gold brocade corset, and a large white veil on her head, opened the door and bowed. So, she asked: "Are you the new owner I have been waiting for?"

"Yes," Mariedda replied, smiling. And from that day on, she was indeed the mistress of the green house hidden in the grove of oranges and roses.

No one ever passed nearby. The world was far away. There was always bread that looked like gold, water like silver, wine like blood, grapes like pearls, flesh like coral, oil like amber, honey like topaz, and milk like snow.

Mariedda was happy. She prayed and waited for the right moment to see her beloved husband. Meanwhile, the beautiful child, called Consiglio, grew like the fruit of the grove. He laughed and played, ran and spun on a cane horse without a tail.

Five years passed.

One day a group of hunters passed by the green house. They were lost in the uninhabited countryside and asked Mariedda for hospitality.

Imagine Mariedda's heartbeat, surprise, and joy when she recognised her husband, I mean, the chief of the lost hunters!

"The big day has come," she thought anxiously.

The men, however, did not recognise her.

In fact, time had changed her. Besides, she was wearing ordinary clothes. So Mariedda remained relaxed and greeted the hunters, including Don Juanne, the devil's doctor.

The hunters were pleased with the hospitality. They also appreciated Mariedda's kindness and Consiglio's beauty.

At the table Don Mariano was sitting next to the woman. Then he told her of his misfortune. He also told her that he regretted sending her away and that he had searched all the mountains and valleys of Sardinia for his poor wife. Unfortunately, he had not found her. For this reason, he was the most unhappy man in the world, tormented by remorse and memories.

Mariedda was moved by this story and decided to reveal herself before the hunters left. In the meantime, this extraordinary event happened, showing how divine justice is revealed in the smallest things.

Listen to me!

A golden spoon fell to the ground. Consiglio, playing between the chairs, picked it up. Then, moving under the table, he put the spoon in Don Juanne's embroidered Moroccan shoe. Then he went to bed. As they cleared the table, the women noticed that the golden teaspoon was missing. They searched everywhere for it but could not find it. "My lord," Mariedda said to the prince, "I have given you and your knights hospitality. Why are you doing this to me?" And so, she told the story of the golden teaspoon, which had undoubtedly been stolen by one of the hunters.

Don Mariano became angry. He drew his sword and shouted, "Knights, someone has stolen something. Confess, or you will regret it!"

Everyone denied it. Then Don Mariano continued: "All right, gentlemen! Who is the author of this unworthy act? Who has betrayed the hospitality of our noble lady? I'll take care of it. And the person responsible will be killed by my sword."

Said, done. He searched all the hunters and found the golden spoon in Don Juanne's embroidered Moroccan shoe.

In vain he said he was innocent. "You will die by my hand," replied the prince. And he wanted to kill him. But

Mariedda begged him not to. So, she revealed herself. And the prince was happy. Don Juanne was moved. He threw himself at the feet of his niece, who had saved him. Then he confessed.

Mariedda and Mariano forgave him. As penance, they ordered him to live only in the little green house hidden among the orange and rose trees. We do not know if he really repented. But we do know that he never left. We also know that Mariedda, Consiglio with her reed horse, the servant girl, Don Mariano and all the other hunters returned to the court, where they were welcomed with great festivities and lived happily ever after.

As they passed by the ponds, the same fisher sang: "Birds that fly, that fly with me, go and return, queen, and king."

## The legend of the birth of the launeddas

An ancient shepherd grazed his flock not far from the sea. It was a very distant time, an almost prehistoric spring. But the landscape was the same as it is today. The cool, green plain overlooking the sea was surrounded by dark mountains and a clear, blue sky. Even the shepherd's hut was the same as it is today. And so was the shepherd. He was old, but still strong. He had long hair, a long yellow beard and black, wrinkled eyes. He was dressed in wool and fur.

The old man's name was Sadur. I do not know the etymology of this name. From this name comes Sadurru, which means Saturnino. He lived with his young wife and their daughter Greca.

On the plain there were other huts where other shepherds lived. But where did these first Sardinians come from, with their little brown women? And with their still wild flocks?

Perhaps their fathers, too, had come in raiding boats from the shores of the East. And I say "too", because sometimes the reddish wing of a Phoenician sail appeared on the silver sea. Then a group of pale men disembarked from the boats. They wore short grey tunics, sandals on their feet and conical caps on their heads. And they spread like a whirlwind across the plain, setting fire to the huts, plundering what they could, slaughtering the sheep and eating under the trees.

Sadur harboured a fierce hatred for these unwelcome visitors who had repeatedly ruined him. Often, he had escaped to the mountains with his family and flock, returning to the plains as the red sails slowly disappeared over the horizon in the purple twilight of the sea. But now he saw his extreme old age approaching painfully. And he felt his strength sadly diminishing.

Who would be the saviour of his family and his flock?

He sat melancholy at the entrance to the sheepfold.

He gazed restlessly at the clear line of the sea.

For a long time, the life of the first Sardinian shepherds was untroubled. Only a few primitive traders came from time to time. They brought wheat, legumes, cloth, dried fruit, ornaments, and bronze jewellery. In return, they received wool, honey, cheese, and sheep's nails. Then they left.

Women ground wheat between two stones, baked cakes and sewed clothes.

Sadur watched the flocks and stared out to sea. Despite the peace of these last years, he was not at peace. His eyes grew weak, his wild teeth moved between his gums, and his hands began to tremble.

Sadur was very sad. His only consolation was often to play certain reed flutes, very crude and primitive.

The result was a monotonous but faint, muted melody, lost like a lament in the great silence.

When he played his reed flutes, Sadur forgot all his sadness. His eyes softened, an expression of tenderness and kindness spread over his whole wild physiognomy.

The melancholy sound filled his heart. Everything seemed sweet to him. He dreamed of Greca being married to a brave young man. He also dreamed of dying peacefully under an oak tree in the April sun, seeing his daughter and wife in safe hands.

He had several flutes. Each time he played, he tried them all, one after the other. Depending on their size, each had a particular sound. And Sadur knew how to make different melodies out of them.

Then, in the last year of his life, this happened to him.

It was May.

One day, while on the seashore, he saw the sails of the Phoenicians not far from the shore.

Trembling, he ran to his wife and daughter. Then he told them, "Unfortunately, what I feared is happening. There is only one way to save us. You two will run away and hide with almost all the sheep. Meanwhile, I will stay here with fifteen or twenty sheep. They will think I live alone. They will only take just two or three sheep to eat. After they have gone, we will be reunited."

The two women made their way to the hiding place. Crying, they pushed the herd towards the mountains. As agreed, the old man stayed behind. He pretended to be almost blind and began to play.

The Phoenicians found him so quiet. They thought he lived alone with the few sheep on the nearby pasture. As he had foreseen, they searched the hut, destroyed it for the fire, slaughtered the sheep and ate the meat.

Some Phoenicians wanted to tie up and beat Sadur. However, the chief of the expedition did not agree.

He was a pale young man with long black hair anointed with perfumed oil.

When the banquet was over, he ordered the old man to play. Sadur took his flutes and played. The young chief stood listening, attentive, thoughtful, almost sad. Suddenly he seemed to be seized by a strange whim. Then he ordered Sadur to play all his flutes together.

"How will I do it?" said the old man.

"Do it or I will have you beaten."

So, the old man looked for some stringy herbs and put together his flutes to create the first of the Sardinian leoneddas. After many attempts, he succeeded in creating a melancholic, harmonious, and discreetly sonorous melody.

In the drowsiness of a spring afternoon, after a hearty meal, the Phoenicians listened as they lay on the grass, and a great sweetness came over them at the sound.

The young man seemed enchanted. Gradually he fell asleep, and it seemed to him that he had never slept so well in a more pleasant place. When he awoke, he told the old man to ask him for anything he wanted; he would grant it if it was in his power.

Sadur trembled, then said: "I have a wife and a virgin daughter. Please, if you meet them, don't touch them".

"You can bring them back here," said the chief, "they will not be molested". Meanwhile, he ordered his men to rebuild the hut and waited for the old man, who had gone to look for his wife and daughter.

He longed to hear the flutes again.

He wanted to sleep on the grass.

The old man came back and played again.

The young man fell asleep.

Then the women and the flocks also returned.

The young man awoke and saw Greca. And everything seemed even more beautiful.

"Will you give me your daughter in marriage?" the chief asked the old man. "I will marry her and stay here with my people".

One of the first Phoenician colonies was thus founded in Sardinia. From then on, the old Sadur played his reed flutes tied together.

## The strange case of Zia Biròra the egg seller

Zia Biròra Portale was an egg seller.

Once she was carrying a basket of eggs from Orotelli to Nuoro. It was an August night, clear and bright as a pearl. The moon shone brightly and evenly over the vast plain of stubble; the sky was almost as blue as at day, and only to the east did the horizon appear vaporous, obscuring the mountains that looked like clouds rising from the sea.

Zia Biròra travelled at night because she walked. And she walked because her income from her trade was very low, and she could not buy a horse.

Imagine that all the capital of her trade, very fragile indeed, was in the basket on her head: two hundred eggs.

So, Zia Biròra left for Nuoro.

She would earn the money to live for three days.

She had been doing this job for years.

In Nuoro, where she sometimes even begged, everyone knew her. But she became even more popular because of the strange case that happened to her that August night.

So, she travelled across the plain, illuminated by the moon, along paths carved in the stubble, in the *tancas*, so melancholy and poetic, completely uninhabited and deserted.

What was she thinking? It is a little difficult to say, because her thoughts were not connected; rather, they were fragments of thought, bits of simple ideas scattered against a colourless background.

Yes, Zia Biròra, who had never been a cheerful woman, felt a great melancholy that night; she was exhausted, sleepy and unable to rest. She was tired of her journey, which had lasted thirty years and never ended. She also had a premonition of an imminent calamity or misfortune; but she never thought it would come so soon – in ten minutes, in a hundred, in ten steps.

Climbing a small hill leading from the fields to the road, the old merchant slipped and fell.

Blum!

The eggs cracked and a cascade of wet straw and white shells poured down the hill. The old woman stood up. She looked pale and dazed, as if she had been hit on the head.

Everything, everything was lost.

She was ruined, forever.

She sat down and began to cry heartily, like a ten-year-old girl. For minutes she was lost in her grief, crying, and moaning loudly, when she heard a sonorous voice echoing behind her.

"Woman!" said the voice, "what has become of you? Why do you frighten the silent travellers of the night with your cries?"

The old woman looked and saw, bathed in the moonlight, a handsome, elegantly dressed young man. On his shoulder he held a fine rifle, its arabesque barrel gleaming.

Zia Biròra thought he was a hunter.

So, she told him about the wretched case.

"For thirty years," she said, "for thirty years I have been travelling, day and night, to earn a crust of bread. Ah, how miserable I am! It had never happened to me to fall but now I am getting old, my legs bend, sleep surprises me. What shall I do now?"

"You have no family?"

"No one, no one. I live alone like the beasts. What will I do now? When I ask for alms, they tell me: Why have you not worked? Ah, do they not know that I have worked harder than any other Christian creature? Do you see my feet? Do you see my feet, young hunter?". And taking one foot with both hands, she turned his palm towards the stranger.

He bent down to look and saw that poor palm of the foot had been reduced to a sort of course, black, cracked leather, stained here and there with blood.

"It's horrible," he muttered to himself, "a poor old woman walking like that."

Zia Biròra was too clever not to take advantage of the traveller's pity. She hoped to get some good charity. So, she went on telling him about her misfortunes, perhaps exaggerating them a little.

He listened thoughtfully, tucking in his chin, which was adorned with a pretty dimple. Suddenly, in the distance, the sound of a horse's hoof broke the silence. Then the stranger took out his wallet from his inside jacket pocket. He took out a note, gave it to the old woman, put the wallet back and disappeared.

It was as if the ground had swallowed him up.

She felt a strange sense of terror, but arcane terror mixed with deep joy. She found herself kneeling, the note in her clasped hands, without realising it.

"He was an angel," she thought, "he was St Michael the Archangel. God be praised, he does not abandon the poor. This must be a twenty-five note: I am saved, my old age is assured. Blessed be St Michael the Archangel. It was him! It was him!"

She dragged herself to her knees. She kissed the ground where the stranger had placed his feet and prayed.

She was found in this position by two villagers passing by on horseback, who thought she had fainted. They called for her and one of them dismounted.

She stood up and told the story, saying that she had seen St Michael the Archangel giving her alms. They thought she was mad, asked to see the note and were astonished to see that it was a "cento lire" note. Then they moved on.

Cento lire! One hundred Sardinian liras!

The old woman thought she was really going mad: she started laughing and crying at the same time, beating her chest, throwing herself on the ground and kissing again the place where the stranger had stopped.

Sometime later, Zia Biròra, who was still selling eggs but on horseback, happened to be in front of the Court in

Nuoro. A famous trial was going on against a bandit accused of murder, robbery, and revenge.

The old woman entered and mingled with the crowd. Suddenly there were shouts, exclamations, and murmurs from the crowd. In short, there was great confusion.

But what had happened?

It was the fault of Zia Biròra, who had recognised her Archangel Michael in the cruel bandit.

## The fairy house and the little silver ring

In Sardinia there are still fairy houses.

These fairies were very small, as small as two-year-old girls. They were called Janas. They were not always good fairies. In fact, they were often very bad. For this reason, there is a curse in the dialect against those who may have done harm: "Mala Jana ti jucat" (a bad fairy will take you or follow you).

My dream as a child was to visit and enter these houses, or domos de Janas. But they were far from the village, usually in deserted, rocky places.

It was not easy.

The stories that a young shepherd told me every time he came to the village to change his shirt and go to church increased my desire.

This servant said that he had visited the Domos de Janas several times.

He described the details in a low voice.

"The door is low and narrow, made of stone slabs. At first you will only see a small room - a cave of stones - where the grass snakes and lizards hide. But if you stay cool, you will find a moving stone that turns like a door. Gotcha! This is the real entrance to the Janas' house. Crawl a little further and you'll soon find yourself in a room over seven metres high, gilded like a pulpit, with a star-studded vault. Then you see thousands of doors opening wide and a series of rooms, each more beautiful than the last, leading to a terrace overlooking the sea".

The last detail was the most intriguing: the mysterious underground house that opened out into the endless breath of the sea. But there was little to believe in what the boy said. He was a visionary, often ill with malaria, and what he dreamed in his delusions he believed to be true.

Thus, he knew a whole range of respectable characters, from the great devil to the goblin Surtòre, who stays in houses where no one sees him, hides objects, incites women to gossip and opens the door to vampires [sùrbiles] who suck the blood of children. He said that, in the solitude of the mountains, he had seen deer led by a shepherd who also had coppery antlers like those of his agile flock.

Well, the shepherd was the devil, and the deer were the souls of thieves.

He told how he had seen a beautiful child by the sea, with golden hair and heavenly eyes, who took sea water in a shell and spread it around, and on the barren sand sprouted wheat and vines; and this child was Jesus!

Giants and dwarves used to visit him when he was alone in the sheepfold watching the sheep, especially on foggy days when it was easier to get away and hide.

Finally, he had a small silver ring with a small pearl (which was then a piece of crystal) in which the seven colours of the iris were reflected. Anyway, he said that after a storm he found the exact spot where the rainbow begins. He dug there and found the ring, which enables those who possess it to invent a hundred and one stories in a single evening.

That little ring was the only concrete proof of what he had said. To make up wonderful stories, you really had to leave him alone.

But that is what happened.

One year, in a September as warm and green as an early spring, we found ourselves in Valverde, a beautiful valley of rocks and bushes, in a lonely stratum of which stands a small church, said to have been built in ancient times by a bandit as a penance and atonement for his sins.

A wonderful place, wonderful days, each one a poem: each hour a verse, each day a harmonious stanza.

And one Sunday, our boy happened to be carrying a candle to Our Lady of the Little Church on behalf of his paralysed grandmother. After praying and placing the candle, he came out and suggested to me and some of my friends that we go with him to see the Domos de Janas, which he said were just a stone's throw away.

So, we set off.

But the two steps were doubled, as in the famous legend: two, four, eight, sixteen, thirty-two, sixty-four, etc. We climbed up and down a steep path. The fairies' houses are there, on that stony hill where some birds flutter and whistle like the wind. To tell the truth, someone is afraid: are those big black birds bad people transformed by fairies?

The boy gives us courage. "Can't you see they're crows? Maybe there is some carrion of a beast or a dead man up there and they are just eating."

A little girl falls and cries.

"In your face!" he says.

"Why have you come without the consent of your parents? You should all fall to the bottom of the valley! Let's go... here we are... here is the door... do you see it? The one between the four stones behind the mastic!"

There is indeed a kind of black hole.

But it's high up, between a pile of rocks, and only birds can get there. What if there is some hidden man, some evildoer who wants to hurt us?

Suddenly we heard a very sharp whistle, as if it were about to blow us away. And the whole gang, including our good guide, stopped.

To show us his courage, the boy goes ahead and answers the whistle with another whistle, as if to say to the hidden enemy:

"If you have courage, come out!". No one responds to the whistle, but rocks fall from above and hit someone.

The birds screeched: "In your faces, little girls, for seeking adventure without your parents' permission."

The boy begins to shout with his hand over his mouth, insulting and calling out to the hidden enemy, then screams to stop and attacks the fortress.

But when he came to the hole, which he believed to be the door of the fairies, a hand treacherously pushed him down, and he rolled like a ball, fortunately without being seriously hurt, but leaving shreds of his clothes in the bushes, and losing his things from his pocket.

Then two hellish brats stood laughing before the hole, and we of the company, ungrateful, mocked our poor guide. They laughed and ran away; even the boy was forced to retreat, for a terrible wave of stones began again, and in his rage, threatening revenge, he did not notice that he had lost the silver ring.

So, I took the silver ring.

And I still have it.

From: *Il dono di Natale*

## Efix and the spirits of the forest

The moon rose before him, and the voices of the evening warned the man that his day was over. It was the cadenced cry of the cuckoo, the sound of the first crickets, the whimper of a bird; it was the sigh of the reeds and the increasingly clear voice of the river; but above all it was a breath, a mysterious gasp that seemed to come from the earth itself. Yes, the day of the labourer was over, but the fantastic life of goblins, fairies and wandering spirits was beginning.

The ghosts of the ancient barons descended from the ruins of the castle above the village of Galte, on the horizon to the left of Efix, and walked along the banks of the river in search of wild boar and fox. Their weapons glittered among the low alders on the bank, and the faint barking of dogs in the distance marked their passage.

Efix heard the noise that the Panas (dead women in childbirth) made when they washed their clothes in the river, beating them with a dead shinbone, and he thought he saw the Ammattadore, a sprite with seven hats in which he hides a treasure, jumping here and there under the almond tree, chased by vampires with steel tails.

It was his passage that made the branches and stones glitter under the moon. Evil spirits were joined by unbaptised children, and white spirits flew and turned into silver clouds behind the moon. And the dwarfs and the janas, little fairies who spend the day in their rock houses weaving golden cloth in golden looms, danced in the shade of the great bushes, while the giants looked out between the rocks of the moon-beaten mountains, holding by the bridle the huge green horses they only know how to ride, to see if a dragon was hiding among the evil euphorbias, or if the legendary serpent Cananèa, who has lived since the time of Christ, was crawling on the sands around the swamp.

Especially on moonlit nights, all these mysterious people enliven the hills and valleys. Man has no right to disturb them with his presence, for the spirits have respected him during the day. It is time to retire and close our eyes under the protection of the guardian angels.

Efix made the sign of the cross and stood up, still waiting for someone to come. However, he pushed open the plank that served as a door and leaned a large reed cross against it to keep the goblins out.

Moonlight poured into the narrow, low room through the slits, illuminating the corners. But the room was wide enough for him, small and skinny as a teenager. From the conical roof of reeds and rushes that covered the dry walls, with a hole in the middle for the smoke to escape, hung bunches of onions and dried herbs, palm crosses and blessed olive branches, a painted candle, a sickle against vampires and a sack of barley against the Panas. Everything trembled with every breath, and the spider threads shone up to the moon. On the floor lay the jar with its straps on its sides, and beside it slept the overturned pot.

From: *Canne al vento*

# Cosima and the Legend of the Mouflon

It was a long and cruel winter, the like of which had never been seen before. First came a great snow that buried the mountains and villages. One night more than a metre of snow fell in front of our house. We had to dig a road to get there without sinking.

At first the children were happy, especially those who had an excuse not to go to school. Andrea made a large, monumental statue in the garden, with two chestnuts for pupils and a fur cap on his head.

Santus tried to go to school instead but had to return because the schools were in an old monastery on the outskirts of town, and the snow was too high to get there. So, the student locked himself in the upstairs room with a Siberian cold and began to study.

The one who had the most fun was Cosima. For the first time, she saw snow in all its terrible beauty, and things seemed infinitely large, transformed into clouds.

Another wonderful sight for her was the fire.

All the fireplaces were lit, as was the central hearth in the kitchen. The flame seemed to come naturally from the floor, bending here and there, curious, and almost eager to break free and run around. The smoke rose to the ceiling and through every opening, but returned as it was repelled by the cold outside. So, the smoke became naughty and disturbed the people.

Fortunately, a servant had returned the day before from the seminerio, the fields where he had sown wheat. Now, stuck in the snow, he stayed at home and helped in a hundred ways: he cut wood under the canopy; he looked after the horse in the stable and the pig and the cold chickens; he looked after the fire; he drew water from the well. Then he also went out to look for meat to make broth. The other supplies were all in the house, and there was no fear, even if the snow lasted for weeks.

Towards evening the snow began to fall again, thick, and steady. Doors and windows were closed and locked, as if against an enemy. So, in the deep silence the voices of the house vibrated like a mountain hut. In the dining room there was a brazier around which the mother and the girls sat.

Cosima tried to take her place among the sisters, but the two elders rejected her as usual and pushed her around, despite her mother's reproaches.

In silence, she made her way to the kitchen. It was perhaps better there, though the smoke still obscured the surroundings. The servant was away from the fire, for a strong man is not and must never be cold, and in imitation Andrea sat beside him, both in two low chairs. Cosima, for her part, sat beside the woman, her head in her lap, a little fat and warm.

The servant was a man of the land. His name was Proto. He was short and stout, with a large, square, reddish beard and greenish eyes. He looked like a monk and was very religious and simple, with an innate Franciscan goodness. The man was always telling stories about saints, although Andrea and Cosima preferred legends or stories about bandits. But for the latter, he left them to the other servant, who was a friend of the refugees and the bandits. So Proto told some long stories and legends to please the children.

"This story - he said that evening - is not made up; it is true, and it happened when I was a child. In my country the winters are longer and harder because we are in the mountains and the shepherds must go down with their flocks to winter in the plains; the women never leave the house; the mouflons come down from the peaks in search of food."

"Even wolves?" Andrea asked.

"No, there are no wolves. We are good people, and animals are good too. There is no animal sweeter than the mouflon, which is a kind of wild goat, but more beautiful and agile than the goat, and harmless. The hunters who hunt it and come from far away are worse than the wildest of them.

Once, one of these good animals, driven by hunger, went down to the last house in the country and wandered around all night.

Now you must know that in that house lived a girl whose boyfriend, a rich shepherd, had gone south for a month. He had caught pneumonia on the way. And now he lay in a distant land, while his servants continued the journey with the flock.

She wanted to reach her boyfriend, but her parents would not let her. She cried all the time and could not sleep at night. Then she heard the slight rustling of the mouflon in the house.

At first she was frightened, thinking they were thieves; then she thought perhaps her friend had died and her spirit, returning to the places of her happiness, was looking for her.

Then she got up and opened the window.

The night was cold but still, without snow. The moon illuminated the profile of the mountain that descended to the house. In this light the girl saw the mouflon, which she searched here and there for food. The animal was graceful, with copper-coloured hair polished by the cold, and big, sweet eyes that sparkled in the moonlight.

She thought: It is surely the spirit of my husband who has taken this form and comes to greet me before he leaves for the other world.

She went down to the ground, but the beast escaped. So, she put on her bonnet and went to the mountain. But the mouflon did not return, and she thought it was not his ghost.

She went back into the house and put a basket of hay and barley on the doorstep. Soon she heard the mouflon munching hungrily.

The next night was no different.

The third night she left the door open and put the basket on the threshold. Sitting by the fire, she saw the beast come in, come out, come in again and eat.

On the fourth night, she put the basket in the kitchen by the wide-open door. The beast took courage and entered. Little by little, they became friends. And the woman began to suffer a little less.

She waited for him every night like a lover, and when he was late, she was worried. She told no one of her adventure to protect the beast. She only told her boyfriend, Alessio, when he returned in good health. But the young man became strangely jealous.

The mouflon no longer came down from the mountains because it was no longer hungry, and in the good times there were people who could hunt it. The girl thought she'd never see the mouflon again. Then, in the autumn, she got married. And in winter the groom left with his flock, his servants, and his dogs.

But that very night, a very cold, frosty night, the mouflon returned. She heard him knocking at the door and went down to open it, her heart pounding as if it were a secret rendezvous.

The story began again: the mouflon was in the kitchen, like a dog, near the fire, and the woman whispered all her secrets to him.

She was not superstitious; she did not believe, like other women in the country, that ghosts, and often even living men, turn into beasts, especially at night. Perhaps she believed in the mouflon's first appearance when she was unhappy about her boyfriend's illness. But now that she was happy again, she thought the mouflon was just an animal. She loved it like a pet. In fact, she wanted to keep it in the house, but not as a prisoner. So, after the usual visit, she opened the door.

And now comes the most important thing.

Her husband came home for Christmas.

She was unsure whether to tell him about her adventure, but she did not hide her fear and, as in the first nights, she left the basket of hay and barley outside the door. The next morning, she found everything intact: a sign that the beast had not come. And she did not return all those nights when her husband stayed at home.

Then a sense of superstition returned to the young woman. There must have been something human about the mouflon. This creature was too intelligent and not just a wild animal. She also thought that someone had killed the mouflon. That's why she was in so much pain.

The husband noticed this and did not know whether to laugh or get angry. There was indeed a voice in the village. It was said that the woman, although she had only been married a few weeks, opened the door at night to a mysterious man who came from far away and walked so as not to be recognised.

Then the young man left. The house was sad without him. The village was all white because of the snow. The woman waited for her boyfriend, but without much hope of seeing him again.

Instead, as if warned by some supernatural instinct, the mouflon returns. She greets him trembling, feeds him, caresses him, feels him throbbing and panting, almost waiting to hear him speak.

And notice that this time the animal is in no hurry to leave. But she is tempted to keep the mouflon in the house. So, what's going on?

Finally, she decides to open the door and the friend goes out. A minute passes. From behind the snow-white wall comes a shot from a rifle and the beast falls. In the silence, dogs barked, and some windows opened. The woman had a premonition, waited for the silence to return, and then left. In the light of the snow, she goes to the wall and finds the mouflon dead, its eyes wide open and still glowing with pain.

She covered him with snow, with her hands, and cried all night. No one spoke of the story. And when the snow melted and the mouflon's clothes were found, everyone thought he had died of hunger and cold. She told no one, not even her husband, when he returned. But something terrible had happened.

In September the young woman gave birth to a child. He was beautiful, with copper-coloured hair and big, sweet eyes like those of a mouflon, but he was deaf and dumb.

Cosima loved the story.

With her head on the servant's lap, she thought she was dreaming. She saw the village of Proto, with the houses covered with axes blackened by time and the mountains sparkling with snow and moon; but above all, she had a deep, almost physical impression of the mystery of the fairy tale, of that final silence, the grave of great and terrible things, the myth of a supernatural justice, the eternal story of error, punishment, and human pain.

From: *Cosima.*

Index

Printed in Great Britain
by Amazon

48166869R00066